DILYS PRICE

NORMAN PRICE

BELLA LASAGNE

JAMES

SARAH

MEET ALL THESE FRIENDS IN BUZZ BOOKS:

Thomas the Tank Engine

The Animals of Farthing Wood

Wind in the Willows

Winnie-the-Pooh

Fireman Sam

First published in Great Britain by Buzz Books,
an imprint of Reed Books, Children's Publishing
Michelin House, 81 Fulham Road, London SW3 6RB
and Auckland, Melbourne, Singapore and Toronto

Fireman Sam © copyright 1985 Prism Art & Design Ltd
Text © copyright 1992 Reed International Books Ltd
Illustrations © copyright 1992 Reed International Books Ltd
Based on the animation series produced by Bumper Films
for S4C/Channel 4 Wales and Prism Art & Design Ltd
Original Idea by Dave Gingell and Dave Jones,
assisted by Mike Young. Characters created by Rob Lee
All rights reserved.
10 9 8 7 6 5 4 3

ISBN 1 85591 212 0

Printed in Italy by Olivotto

THE FAIRGROUND RESCUE

Story by Rob Lee
Illustrations by The County Studio

A fun fair had come to Pondypandy and everybody was enjoying themselves.

"I'll treat you ladies to a toffee apple," said Trevor to Dilys and Bella.

"Let's go on the helter skelter, Mam!" cried Norman.

"Not me!" replied Dilys. "Just the thought of it makes me go all dizzy."

"I'll take you, Norman," said Fireman Sam.

"Can we come too?" asked the twins.

"Of course," chuckled Fireman Sam. "Let's go."

On the way, Fireman Sam and the children stopped to buy ice-creams.

"Yummee! It's fantastic," drooled Norman, licking the drips round his cone.

"Last one to the top's a cissy!" cried Sarah, when they reached the helter skelter.

"Wheeee!" squealed the twins as they sped down the slide. Norman slid down so fast his ice-cream flew right out of the cone!

Meanwhile, Dilys and Bella were enjoying
a ride on the ferris wheel.

"We're so high up people down below
look like ants," said Dilys.

"Ah, bellissimo," sighed Bella. "I haven't
done this since I was a little girl in Roma."

Down below, Fireman Sam suggested
a ride on the roller coaster next.

"Brill!" replied Sarah.

"Why don't you come too, Trevor?"
asked James.

"Not likely!" replied Trevor. "I can't stand
heights. This is more my style!" he grinned,
climbing onto a carousel horse.

As Trevor enjoyed his ride on the carousel,
Fireman Sam and the children climbed
aboard a roller coaster car.

"Hold on tight," said Sam as the car
moved off slowly and began climbing a
steep stretch of track.

"This is boring!" moaned Norman. "It's
much too slow!"

Soon the car reached the crest of the track. Suddenly, it began speeding down the other side. Faster and faster it went!

"Whooa!" cried Norman.

"You don't seem so bored now, Norman!" laughed Fireman Sam.

"Wheeee!" squealed the twins. "This is brill Uncle Sam!"

Dilys and Trevor watched from below as Fireman Sam and the children raced up and down at high speed.

The car reached the top of a hill, then suddenly stopped. Fireman Sam looked down at the cars at the bottom of the roller coaster. They weren't moving either.

On the ground below, Trevor and Dilys
were puzzled.

"What's happened?" asked Dilys.

"I'm not sure," said Trevor. "I'm going to
check the control booth. You call the
fire brigade!"

Trevor raced over to the control booth. It was just as he'd feared – the roller coaster had had a power failure and Sam and the children were stranded at the top!

From the top of the track, Fireman Sam could see Trevor beside the control booth.

"Great fires of London!" he cried. "I do believe there's been a power cut."

"But how will we get down?" asked James.

"Don't worry," said Sarah, "Uncle Sam's sure to think of something."

Sam frowned. All he could think of was to call the Pontypandy Fire Brigade. But how could he from the top of the roller coaster?

"Everybody stay very still until help arrives," said Fireman Sam.

"It's a l-long way down," gulped James.

"M-Miles," stuttered Norman.

From down below, Trevor shouted, "Don't move, Sam. We've called the fire station!"

As Fireman Sam breathed a sigh of relief, Jupiter raced into the fun fair, followed closely by Venus, their lights flashing and sirens blaring.

"Jump to it!" commanded Station Officer Steele, as the engines screeched to a halt.

"Get the equipment from the lockers," ordered Station Officer Steele. "Firefighter Cridlington, we'll have to cordon off the area, and make sure the passengers in the cars at the bottom of the track get off safely!"

"Yes, sir!" replied Elvis.

Meanwhile, Firefighter Penny Morris began unloading ladders from Jupiter.

They leaned the ladders against the roller coaster. "It's no use," said Station Officer Steele. "Sam's car is too high for the ladders to reach."

"Why don't we lean them onto the lowest part of the roller-coaster and then use the catwalk?" suggested Penny.

"Good idea," replied Station Officer Steele.

The children watched nervously from the roller coaster car as Station Officer Steele and Firefighter Penny Morris began climbing the ladders.

"I wish they'd hurry. I don't like it up here," said Norman.

At last Station Officer Steele and Penny climbed onto the catwalk. A few minutes later they reached the car.

"Thank goodness," whispered James.

"Is everyone all right?" asked Penny.

The children nodded their heads.

Fireman Sam lifted the children out of the car one by one and the firefighters took them down the catwalk to safety.

"Is my brave little darling all right?" cooed Dilys anxiously as Norman reached the bottom of the ladder.

"Huh!" replied Norman. "I wasn't scared at all, Mam."

"Not much!" chuckled Sarah and James.

Sarah turned to Fireman Sam. "I knew you'd think of a plan, Uncle Sam."

"Me?" said Fireman Sam. "I didn't do anything. It was the quick thinking of Trevor and Dilys and the expert help of the Fire Brigade that rescued us."

"Thank you, everyone," said the children.

"I'll tell you one thing, I'll be keeping my feet on the ground from now on," added James.

"Excellent job," Station Officer Steele said proudly.

"Yes, I think everyone deserves a treat, Sir," said Sam. "And what better place to have one than a fun fair!"

"That's a grand idea," chuckled Station Officer Steele. "Let's have some fun!"

First, Station Officer Steele and Dilys had a ride on the log flume. Unfortunately, when their log landed in the pool it made a hugh splash and poor old Trevor got soaked!

27

"Let's go on the dodgems now!" cried Sarah and James.

"Not me!" chuckled Fireman Sam. "I've had quite enough excitement for one day!"

"And I'm too wet," moaned Trevor.

So Penny, Elvis and the children roared around in their dodgem cars, laughing as they bumped into each other.

Meanwhile, Fireman Sam wandered off to the snack kiosk and returned with a huge hot dog for Trevor.

"Here you are, Trev. This may not dry you off, but it will certainly cheer you up," said Sam. "You deserve it."

"Thanks, Sam," said Trevor, licking his lips. "That's what I call the fun of the fair!"

FIREMAN SAM

STATION OFFICER
STEELE

TREVOR EVANS

ELVIS
CRIDLINGTON

PENNY MORRIS